*Primitive man gazed up at the stars and both
wondered and speculated what might lie out there in
outer space. Since that time, man has probed further
and further, discovering more and more about our own
galaxy and others. This book not only charts that
fascinating story, it also anticipates the information that
may come back to us from spacecraft that will still be
travelling in the last years of the 20th and even into the
21st century.*

Acknowledgments

The author and publishers wish to acknowledge the use of additional
illustrative material as follows:

Cover – Jeremy Flack, Aviation Photographs International, and
Armagh Planetarium; pages 4, 10, 11 (two), 12, 13, 14, 15, 16, 17, 18,
23 (two), 24, 25, 26, 27, 28, 30, 33, 35, 36, 38, 39, 40 (two), 45, 51 –
Armagh Planetarium; page 6 – Anne Buxton; back cover and pages 5,
19 (two), 29 (two), 32, 34, 46, 48, 49 – Daily Telegraph Colour
Library, copyright Space Frontiers Ltd; pages 7, 8, 9 – Novosti Press
Agency; pages 20 and 21 – Popperfoto; page 31 – Space and New
Concepts Department, R A E Farnborough; page 50 – Science Photo
Library.

British Library Cataloguing in Publication Data
Murtagh, Terence
    Space.—(Achievements. Series 601; no. 9)
    1. Space flight—History—Juvenile literature
    I. Title   II. Series
    629.4′1′09   TL793
    ISBN 0-7214-0832-X

First edition

© LADYBIRD BOOKS LTD MCMLXXXIV

Space

by Terence Murtagh
illustrated by Gerald Witcomb MSIAD

Ladybird Books Loughborough

Exploring Space

In late August of 1989, a large ungainly spacecraft will swoop a few thousand kilometres above the green cloud tops of the planet Neptune. At that time, Neptune will be the world which is furthest away from our Sun.

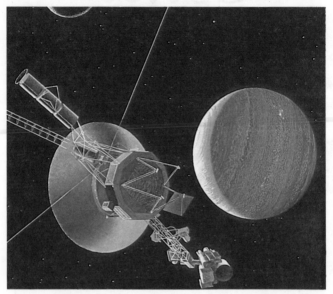

Voyager spacecraft on its journey through space

That spacecraft, known as *Voyager 2*, will be an 808 kg robot explorer which was sent out from Earth in 1977. It will have been travelling through the solar system for almost one-third of the space age, which began on 4th October 1957 with the launch of the first man-made moon or satellite.

For thousands of years people from Earth have studied the planets. At first all they could see was a series of bright star-like lights moving across the sky.

The planet Saturn photographed by Voyager 2

Then gradually it was realised that these moving objects called planets travelled around our Sun in almost circular paths or *orbits*. Our own world, the Earth, was just one amongst many such planets in the Sun's family which we call the *solar system*.

When the telescope was invented – nearly four hundred years ago – it became possible to see the planets much more clearly. We could see that they were worlds – some with hazy markings, some with brilliant white clouds, and others with colourful swirling belts and puzzling rings. Still others had possible white icecaps.

We were exploring our own world, and now we wanted to reach out and explore these strange worlds as well. But the more we learned, the less possible it seemed that we would ever reach these places, except in our imagination.

Rockets and Missiles

Some people dreamed and wondered just what those new worlds were like. Others however were thinking about the machines that would be needed to get there.

Three men laid the foundations for the present space age. They were Konstantin Tsiolkovsky in Russia, Robert Goddard in America, and Hermann Oberth in Romania.

They knew that only a rocket could travel in space, and that this would provide our stepping stone into the unknown.

Once beyond the thin shell of the Earth's atmosphere, other vehicles couldn't operate. Without air, an aircraft's wings would no longer support it, and without oxygen its engines couldn't burn their fuel. A rocket however could carry its own oxygen and fuel into the

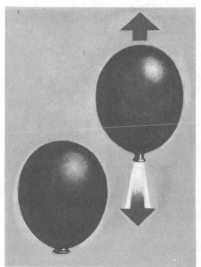

When you watch a rocket taking off, you may think that it is propelled by the gas from its exhausts pushing against the air. It is not, however – a rocket obeys the scientific law which states that for every action there is an equal and opposite reaction. With a rocket engine, when the gas escapes through the exhaust, it exerts an equal force in the opposite direction. When you blow up a balloon, then release the air from it, it will fly across the room in obedience to that same law

vacuum of space, and work very efficiently.

To start with, the rocket pioneers were mostly ignored. Then came the Second World War, when powerful rockets were developed, particularly by Von Braun and his team in Germany, to carry explosives to cities like London.

During the 1950s, much more powerful rockets were being developed in Russia and America. These rockets could hop into space and return to Earth many thousands of kilometres from their launch site.

Vostok launch vehicle, showing the two-stage rocket booster liquid propellant engines

Then scientists realised that if such powerful rockets were launched into space at a speed of about 7 kilometres a second, part of the rocket – or the whole machine – would be travelling so fast that it would never fall down to Earth at all. It would be travelling fast enough to balance the Earth's gravitational pull, and it would simply continue to circle the planet, becoming an artificial moon or satellite.

The first artificial Earth satellite was a simple sphere, about 75 kilograms in weight, launched by the Russians. That was followed soon after by a series of heavier and yet heavier satellites. By 1958 the Americans had their first satellite in orbit and over the next few years the first living creatures, dogs and monkeys, travelled into space. Some returned safely, so that the way was open for the first manned space voyage.

A model of the first artificial Earth satellite

A Russian test pilot journeyed around the world and into history in 108 minutes on the morning of 12th April 1961. He was Yury Gagarin, the world's first space traveller.

Gagarin's launcher was a Vostok rocket: a huge vehicle made up of four conical booster rockets attached to a central core rocket. When the core rocket and satellite have accelerated to their maximum speed, the boosters fall away. Once the fuel is used up, the empty rockets would just slow the vehicle down.

The manned part of the space vehicle was a spherical capsule about 2 metres across. It was covered by a layer of material which slowly burnt and flaked away. This was to protect the astronaut from the searing heat of re-entry as the spacecraft plunged back into the Earth's atmosphere to land.

The Vostok booster and its improved successors have been the main launcher for Russian space missions ever since. The Vostok capsule was used for a number of one-man flights, but on some later missions, as many as three astronauts were squeezed in.

It was however never really designed for multi-crew use, and was later superseded by the much superior Soyuz.

The assembly of the Vostok spaceship

Mercury

In the early days of spaceflight, many of the first spectacular flights were accomplished by the Russians. At last the United States decided that their manned space programme was going to beat the Russians. They were going to land a man on the moon.

The first US manned flight was on 5th May 1961, when Alan Shepard made a fifteen minute hop into space in a Mercury spacecraft.

It was almost a year later that John Glenn became the first American to orbit the Earth. His launcher was the Atlas rocket, which was substantially less powerful than the Russian Vostok.

The Mercury capsule was also different. Technically it was much more advanced than Gagarin's, but it could still only orbit the Earth. The capsule was shaped like a large cone, and was just big enough for a man to squeeze inside. It had an observation window and re-entry protection (a 'heat shield') on the bottom of the cone.

When the capsule was safely through the upper atmosphere, a parachute opened, slowing the spacecraft down to land in the sea. The Russian capsules came down on land, but most of their astronauts ejected and landed separately by parachute.

A Mercury spacecraft takes off

Gemini

1965 saw the first two-manned Vostok flight. During this flight one of the astronauts, Aleksey Leonov, stepped out into the vacuum of space. Encased in his space suit he was a mini space capsule, secured to his mothercraft only by a sturdy lifeline.

Just a few days later the American Gemini programme got under way. *Gemini* was a specially designed two-manned capsule.

More advanced technically than the Vostok or Mercury, it was a large cone with two special doors. Through these doors astronauts could go out into space and practise EVA (extra vehicular activity). This helped later when people were training to walk on the moon.

(above) *The launch of* Gemini 10
(below) *Walking in space*

Gemini *manoeuvring in space*

Gemini could be manoeuvred as well. It could be moved in orbit and could be brought close to other manned spacecraft or linked up with some unmanned vehicles.

Some of these unmanned vehicles were Agena rockets, whose engines were fired, taking *Gemini* many hundreds of kilometres into space. Practising these rendezvous and docking techniques was vital to the plans being developed for Apollo – the first manned flights to the moon.

Apollo

The manned phase of the Apollo programme got off to a truly disastrous start. Three of the first astronauts died in a fire in their Apollo craft, during a pre-launch test in 1967.

This set back the manned Lunar Mission by about two years, but in the long term it led to a much safer spacecraft. In 1967 the Russians also suffered a major setback in their manned programme. One of their astronauts, Vladimir Komarov, was killed when his faulty Soyuz spacecraft plummeted to Earth. Its parachutes had failed to open.

The first manned Apollo flight was in the autumn of 1968, when three astronauts circled the Earth. In the meantime the giant Saturn 5 moon rocket tests proved that it would be safe for a manned mission, *Apollo 8*.

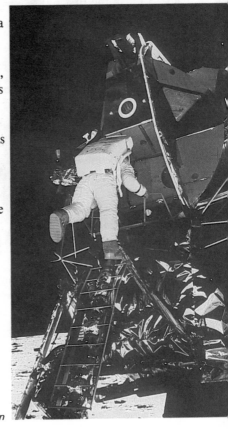

Lunar mission

At last, in December 1968, *Apollo 8* took off for a journey around the moon. The mission over Christmas was a spectacular success, and the astronauts brought back to Earth the first colour pictures taken close to the moon.

Apollo 8 merely circled the moon, but it did prove that the complete system worked. However, there was still one piece of the equipment left untested. That was the actual vehicle that was to land on the moon, known as the Lunar Excursion Module or LEM.

Apollo 9 tried the LEM in Earth orbit. Then *Apollo 10* tested it above the moon, and actually swooped to within 14 kilometres of the lunar surface.

Apollo 11 *is launched*

14

On 16th July 1969, a huge Saturn 5 rocket blasted off from the Kennedy Space Centre in Florida. On a pillar of fire, it slowly climbed into the sky. Soon its three passengers were en route, heading for a spot in space almost 400,000 kilometres distant.

It was known that this was the spot to which the moon would be close in three days' time. The aim was not to hit the moon, but to miss it by a few tens of kilometres.

The moon travels around the Earth at the speed of 3000 kilometres an hour and this had been taken into account. If the rocket had been fired at the moon's position on 16th July, the moon would have been long gone by the time the Apollo spacecraft had reached that spot.

Apollo astronauts being recovered after splashdown

Russian moon probes

Although up to the end of 1968 it was thought that the Russians would launch a manned lunar probe, or at least a manned flight around the moon, they never attempted to do so.

Instead, in the middle of the American manned lunar programme, they launched a series of robot spacecraft which conducted some useful lunar experiments over a period of years.

In September 1970 *Luna 16* was the first successful Russian probe to land on the moon. It collected a sample of about 100 grams of lunar soil, returning it to Earth in a tiny spherical spacecraft.

Russian space probe

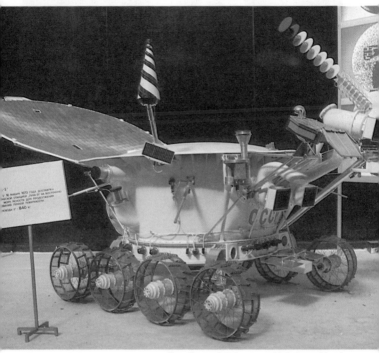

Russian robot lunar vehicle Lunokhod

Later that year *Luna 17* reached the moon's surface. It landed an eight-wheeled robot vehicle *Lunokhod*. Controlled from Earth, *Lunokhod* had two television eyes, and travelled about 10.5 kilometres across the moon over a period of eleven months. It ran in and out of lunar craters, examined rocks, and provided varied views of the lunar plains.

The samples returned by the Russian unmanned vehicles were tiny in comparison to those retrieved by the Apollo programme. Weight for weight they were probably many times more expensive to obtain.

One of the first men on the moon

When the Apollo spacecraft neared the moon, one of its rocket motors was fired. This slowed the spacecraft down so that it could be captured by the moon's gravitational pull and start circling in a lunar orbit.

Two of the three astronauts now climbed out of the cone-shaped Apollo command module into the lunar excursion module. It looked like a giant silver and gold space spider, with four spindly legs. It didn't have to be as sturdy as it would have had to be on Earth, because objects on the moon weigh only one-sixth of what they would on Earth. Also, as it didn't have to fly through an atmosphere, it could have a purely functional shape.

Exploring the moon

Having checked the spacecraft systems, the astronauts in the module undocked from the main craft. Then they went slowly into a new orbital path which would allow them to skim much closer to the surface.

On 20th July 1969 the *Apollo 11* lunar module gently descended onto the moon's surface. Within a few hours the first man, Neil Armstrong, had set foot on the moon, to be followed shortly after by the second, Edwin Aldrin. The exploration of the moon had begun.

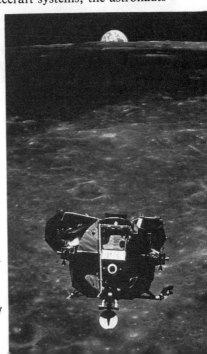

Earthrise on the moon!

Lunar buggy

But that exploration was destined to be a short-lived affair, and only twelve men have walked on the moon's dusty rock-strewn surface.

Apollo 17 in December, 1972, was the last manned lunar mission, bringing a truly exciting phase of space exploration to an end.

In the three years between the first and last lunar landing astronauts had walked, hopped and even driven a special car, a lunar buggy, across the moon. More than 363 kilograms of rock and soil samples had been collected, both from the low flat plains and from the bright highland areas, and returned to Earth.

A network of automatic nuclear powered research stations transmitted information to Earth for many years on moonquakes, surface temperatures on the moon, meteor impacts there, etc.

The lunar samples suggested that the moon had never been part of Earth, and that it had a tortured history of volcanic activity for thousands of millions of years. The samples also showed that most lunar craters were definitely the result of bombardment by massive meteors during the early history of the solar system. It became clear too that the moon had never had an atmosphere like that of the Earth. Its surface had always been bleak and devoid of life – until Man arrived in the second half of the twentieth century.

Moon rock

Mercury

Mercury – like the other bright planets – has been known to man for thousands of years. It appears in our sky as a tiny star-like point either just shortly after sunset or just before sunrise. This is because Mercury is very close to the Sun. It takes only about eighty eight days to go around the Sun once at an average distance of 58 million kilometres.

Mariner 10

It was to be 1974 however before we knew what Mercury was really like. It was in that year the American spacecraft *Mariner 10* went into a solar orbit that meant it could fly past Mercury no less than three times in twelve months. *Mariner's* photographs show that Mercury's wrinkled surface is almost completely splattered with craters of all sizes.

We know that Mercury is a small planet just 4850 kilometres across. This means that it has no atmosphere, because its gravitational pull is not enough to stop any gases which surround it from drifting off into space.

Mercury's surface seen in close-up

And since Mercury has no atmosphere to insulate its surface from the Sun's heat, the temperature can swing wildly. It can go from a daytime high of 510°C to a night-time low of −210°C. So it wouldn't be the most comfortable place to visit!

The planet Mercury

Venus

Like Mercury, Venus travels between the Sun and the Earth.

So it is visible either before dawn or after dusk in the same way. It was sometimes called the 'Morning' and 'Evening' star before people began to find out how the planets moved.

Today we know that Venus, like all the planets, travels around the Sun in an almost circular path or *orbit*. It takes Venus 225 Earth days to go around the Sun once. At an average distance of 108 million kilometres, it is the second planet from the Sun.

In size Venus is just slightly smaller than the Earth. Like the Earth, it also has an atmosphere and is covered with white clouds. They reflect light, the light of the Sun, which means that Venus can be the brightest object in our sky apart from the Sun and the moon. It also comes closer to the Earth than any other planet – only a mere 38 million kilometres away at its nearest point.

The planet Venus

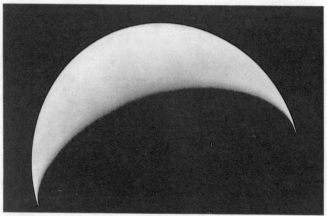

Venus's cloudy atmosphere is made of poisonous gases (photographs taken by Pioneer spacecraft)

Since the telescope was first invented people have been trying to see the surface of Venus, but its cloudy atmosphere has always kept it hidden from view.

In recent years however spacecraft, and radar bounced from Earth, have enabled us to take a look through the clouds and discover what lies below.

It is almost completely different from Earth. The bright clouds have turned out to be composed largely of carbon dioxide, which for us is a poisonous gas. At lower levels, there are probably almost continuous showers of sulphuric acid rain.

We know now that the clouds act rather like the glass on a greenhouse. They let the heat from the Sun come in, but don't let it out again. This means that the surface of Venus is very hot indeed, with a temperature of 470°C.

Lastly, the atmosphere is very thick – much thicker than our own Earth – and with a pressure ninety times as great. That means that even a slight breeze on Venus would feel like a giant hurricane!

The only views of the surface of Venus which we have seen were sent back by planetary probes in the Russian Venera series. Some views showed rocks and boulders, others showed a light soil with rocky outcrops.

Radio waves sent from Earth and bounced back from the surface of Venus told us that a day on Venus lasts 243 Earth days – longer than its year. Another strange thing is that unlike all the other major planets, Venus spins from East to West, in what astronomers call a retrograde fashion. No one knows yet why this is.

Using information provided by this radio reflection technique, maps of Venus's surface have now been drawn. They show that the surface of Venus has only two major continent-sized regions, unlike Earth.

There is also evidence to show that there are large craters on Venus as well as one or two active volcanoes.

Before we knew what Venus was really like, it used to be thought that Venus could be the twin of Earth. Now however we know that Venus is much more of an ugly sister than anything else!

Close-up of Aphrodite Terra, on the surface of Venus – an artist's impression, based on radar results

Earth

We are the first generation of people ever to have seen our own world from a distance as a planet from space.

Earth from space

Satellites now in orbit round Earth give us close-up views of the Earth's weather systems. Other weather satellites further away, orbiting once a day, show us what is happening over the whole planet.

As this weather information is in daily use, it helps with agriculture, and helps to prevent damage from snow storms, floods, hurricanes and typhoons. Yet just thirty years ago, such machines only belonged in science fiction.

Other satellites perched high above the Earth's equator transmit telephone calls and television pictures from one side of the world to the other, at the speed of light. Through the telephone and television, the most distant parts of the Earth have been brought right into people's homes.

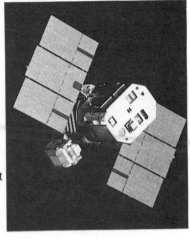

Solar Max, *a satellite used to study the Sun*

Aircraft in flight, ships cruising the oceans – and even individual explorers – can now use navigational satellites to show them exactly where they are on the Earth to within a few metres.

In some ways our world has shrunk, but perhaps because that has happened, our awareness of it has grown. We are beginning to realise that we must look after its natural resources and all its forms of life much better than we have done in the past. It is important both for ourselves and for future generations.

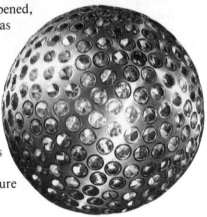

A geodynamic satellite, used to study the real shape of the Earth

At one time people imagined that the Earth lay in the centre of the Universe, and was the most important object in existence. Nowadays we know that ours is only a tiny planet orbiting an ordinary star, but it is indeed the most important body in the Universe for us. Nowhere else has yet been discovered with the necessary atmosphere and conditions to sustain life as we know it.

Think of our Earth as a spaceship, and ourselves as its passengers. The life-giving atmosphere provides a thin protective shell around us as we speed around the Sun at 96,000 kilometres per hour. Our Sun is itself travelling through the Milky Way galaxy at a speed of 19 kilometres per second. So all of us here on Earth are quite seasoned space travellers!

Ours is the third planet from the Sun. It is a modest sized world 12,756 kilometres across. It spins round once in twenty four hours – a period of time which we call a 'day'.

Meteor scar seen from space

It takes the Earth just over 365 days to go once round the Sun – and we call that a 'year'. Over two-thirds of the Earth is covered with water, which is why it looks so blue when viewed from space.

The Earth's weather and the bulk of its atmosphere are in a tight shell about 8 kilometres thick. In the distant past, the

A weather satellite photograph of a depression

Earth's atmosphere was different, even poisonous. Gradually the action of plants changed its composition to that of today: almost four-fifths nitrogen and one-fifth oxygen, with the small balance made up of carbon dioxide, argon and neon.

The Earth is like a giant magnet, with a magnetic field which stretches far into space. This is important to us, because that magnetic field acts like a huge shield, protecting us from harmful radiations which come from the Sun.

Mars

Seen from Earth, Mars is a bright blood-red star. This led to its association with war and hence its naming after the ancient war god of the Romans.

Of all the planets Mars is the best known, largely because of the science fiction stories and films featuring it. Many of these were produced long before spacecraft visited Mars, and were based on observations made through Earth-based telescopes. These showed a red disc with changeable dark areas and white polar caps, and there was great speculation as to what forms of life could live there.

The planet Mars photographed by Viking 1

It is amazing just how wrong our ideas of Mars were! The Mars of science fact has turned out to be very different from the Mars of science fiction. It is however in many ways much more fascinating.

It was when the space age arrived with a series of Mars flybys, orbiters and landers that we found out what things were really like on the red planet.

 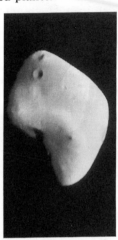

Mars' satellites – Phobos and Deimos

Our most recent knowledge has come mostly from the *Viking* spacecraft which arrived at Mars in 1976. Two craft were put into orbit round the planet, and mapped the surface in detail. Each orbiter carried a lander, and after careful studies of the landing sites from orbit, these were sent down to the surface.

Plunging through the thin Martian air, and protected by a heat shield, the *Viking* landers descended to their targets. They went first by parachute and then more gently by means of tiny rocket engines.

The first landing took place on 20th July 1976. That was just seven years after the Apollo moon landing. As the *Viking* cameras slowly moved along, the bleak rock-strewn and red surface of Mars was revealed.

Viking carried instruments to discover what the Martian atmosphere was like, and to take readings of the temperature, wind speed and direction. It was our own weather station on Mars!

Viking was soon reporting that the Martian air is very thin – about 100 times thinner than Earth's – it is mostly carbon dioxide with just a tiny trace of nitrogen, oxygen and water vapour. It would be extremely unsuitable for most life as we know it.

The surface of Mars, taken from Viking 2

Olympus Mons, on Mars – probably the biggest volcano in the solar system

It is quite cold as well. Even on the warmest days it is distinctly chilly, and at night the temperature plunges to $-100°C$. In winter the surface is covered by a thin layer of carbon dioxide frost.

The *Viking* spacecraft also carried instruments to search for signs of life and tiny organisms. Although a few suggested that something interesting might be going on, the results were almost completely negative. So at the moment it seems that, as far as we can tell, Mars is a lifeless world.

The red planet is just over half the size of the Earth, at 6787 kilometres across. It has a day of twenty four and a half hours, but the Martian year is almost twice as long as ours, at 687 Earth-days. This is because Mars takes longer than Earth to complete one journey round the Sun, since it is much further away from it.

In many ways Mars is still a mysterious and exciting world; it could be an interesting place for a future space holiday!

Jupiter

In the year 1609, Galileo turned his first telescope on the sky, and was amazed to see that Jupiter was circled by four bright moons.

Jupiter (top right) *and its four moons*

Nothing more was found out about these objects for the next three hundred years or more. Then in the last quarter of the twentieth century a telescope aboard a spacecraft called *Voyager* told us a great deal very quickly.

Jupiter itself is the largest of the planets. It is big enough, at 142,800 kilometres across, to fit over one thousand Earths inside it. And it weighs more than twice as much as all the other planets put together.

At 800 million kilometres from the Sun, it takes Jupiter almost twelve Earth-years to go around the Sun once. It is the first of the giant gas planets, which are quite different from the four small rocky worlds huddling closer to the Sun.

Jupiter looks somewhat flattened in pictures because it spins very rapidly. Its day is just under ten hours long. Because it is a big ball of gas, the high speed forces the central regions out and makes it look squat.

The first really good views of Jupiter, its cloud belts, and moons were sent back to Earth by the *Voyager* spacecraft, two of which whizzed past the giant planet in 1979. Now at last the belts and weather systems could be seen in great detail.

The giant bands of cloud were found to be zones of hot and cold gas. These rise as they are heated in the planet's interior and move to the surface, appearing as the lighter zones. As they grow cool they descend, forming the darker belts.

The temperature and chemical range on Jupiter is immense. At the top of the atmosphere it is about −150°C, whereas down in the clouds it gets up to +75°C. Underneath this turbulent atmosphere of hydrogen and helium is an immense ocean of liquid hydrogen, which may surround a small rocky core just slightly larger than the Earth.

In many photographs of the upper atmosphere, a giant red eye can be seen. It is a slowly rotating swirl of gas, coloured red by the action of sunlight on gases from deeper in the atmosphere.

Galileo saw four moons or satellites, but more have now been discovered. The total is now sixteen, in addition to a ring of fine dust particles discovered by *Voyager*. Some of Jupiter's moons are big enough to qualify as small planets!

Jupiter's moons

The four largest, Io, Europa, Ganymede and Callisto can easily be seen from Earth through binoculars. They provided some of the most interesting discoveries made by *Voyager*.

Jupiter's satellite Io, which has been discovered to have active volcanoes

Io is a world slightly bigger than our moon. Its vivid orange and yellow surface looks rather like a cosmic pizza!

It is covered in huge volcanoes throwing not molten rock as on Earth, but molten sulphur. Io appears to be locked in a tug of war between the giant mother planet and another moon, Europa. The contradictory gravitational pull both squeezes and pushes Io so that enormous heat is generated for the massive volcanic system.

A close-up of Europa

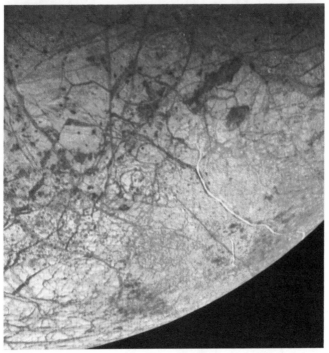

Europa is smaller than Io. It looks quite smooth like a gigantic snooker ball, but it is covered in brownish lines. It has a small rocky core surrounded by a frozen ocean of ice.

Ganymede may be the largest moon in the solar system, with an old icy surface crust about 100 kilometres thick. This probably surrounds a slushy ocean 800 kilometres deep covering a rocky core.

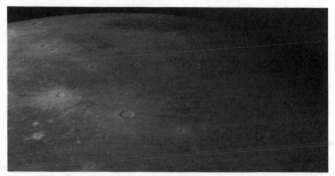

Jupiter's satellite Ganymede, photographed from a quarter of a million kilometres away

Although Callisto is smaller than Ganymede, it is very like it. It bears a strange scar however of a huge impact millions of years ago. At some time in the long-distant past, its icy surface was melted and later refrozen, preserving this great scar on its surface.

A close-up of Callisto

Saturn

Like Jupiter, the planet Saturn is a giant gas ball, 120,000 kilometres across. It is so far from the Sun that it takes twenty nine and a half years to complete one journey round it. Since it spins quickly, with a day of ten and a quarter hours, it looks flattened at the top and bottom just as Jupiter does.

Saturn and some of its satellites

When Saturn was visited by the two *Voyager* spacecraft, they sent back pictures of its satellites, clouds and the unusual rings that circle it.

Saturn's strange and beautiful rings

Before *Voyager*, we thought Saturn had six or seven rings, but now we know that there are thousands. Every ring is made up of particles of dust-covered ice, from dust-sized specks to boulders.

The main ring system encircles Saturn out to a distance of 270,000 kilometres. The rings however are only a few kilometres deep – when they are turned edge-on to the Earth, they can hardly be seen.

Voyager also revealed that like Jupiter, Saturn has a very active weather system. It is however covered by a layer of haze. The atmosphere is a foggy mixture of hydrogen and helium, with smaller amounts of methane and ammonia. Under this is an immensely deep ocean of liquid hydrogen. Very deep down the hydrogen is so compressed that it behaves like a liquid metal and in the centre of Saturn is a rocky core, a solid planet just bigger than the Earth. That core however is inside a layer of liquid gas more than 57,000 kilometres deep!

All this means that Saturn is not a very dense world. It would float if you could find a bowl of water big enough!

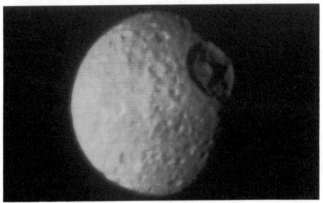

Two of Saturn's seventeen known satellites:
Mimas, showing a huge crater on its surface (above);
and a close-up of Dione (below)

Uranus, Neptune and Pluto

In early 1986 one of the *Voyager* spacecraft which flew past Jupiter and Saturn will fly past the planet Uranus. It will be the first spacecraft to visit this world and, hopefully, send back some information about it.

Uranus is another gas giant about 52,000 kilometres across. We know that it has a series of dark rings although they can never be seen from Earth.

Uranus is so far away from the Sun – 2870 million kilometres – that it takes the planet eighty four years to complete one orbit! Out at this distance most of the solar system is empty space for the next planet, Neptune, is 4500 million kilometres from the Sun.

Neptune, like Uranus, is a gas giant. The gas is a composition of hydrogen, helium and methane, as is that of Uranus. A year on Neptune is almost twice as long as Uranus, lasting nearly 165 Earth-years.

Voyager 2, having passed Uranus in 1986, is due to visit Neptune in 1989. As well as photographs of the planet, we should also get our first views of Neptune's giant satellite, Triton. We believe it may be bigger than the planet Mercury.

Our most recent information about Pluto, usually thought of as the most distant planet, suggests that it may not really be a planet at all. It may have to be thought of as a large double asteroid. This is because Pluto's moon, Charon, is about one-third the size of Pluto itself, which may be only 2400 kilometres across.

Pluto and Charon are probably made of a rock and ice mixture, which is possibly covered by a layer of methane ice. They take 247 years to go around the Sun once. Since their orbit is inside that of Neptune at the moment,

Neptune is for the time being the most distant world in our solar system, and will be so until March 1999.

The spacecraft Voyager 2 *on its way to orbit Uranus in 1986* (artist's impression)

The Space Shuttle

Twenty years to the day from the first manned space flight, a unique new spacecraft headed aloft from the Kennedy Space Centre in Florida.

12th April 1981 was the date of the maiden flight of the space shuttle – the first re-usable space vehicle. At first glance it looks like an aircraft, which it is. It is however also a spacecraft – a space taxi to take men and equipment into and out of Earth orbit.

The launch

The shuttle itself is 37.2 metres long, and for launch into space it uses three of its own engines plus two strap-on solid boosters.

A huge strap-on fuel tank provides liquid hydrogen and oxygen for the three main shuttle engines. These, together with its own on-board rocket engine, thrust the shuttle into orbit.

At a point agreed beforehand, the strap-on boosters fall away from the orbiter. They then parachute to the sea, where they are recovered for re-use. The orbiter continues into space, and jettisons the fuel tank just before going into orbit. The empty fuel tank is burnt up and destroyed as it re-enters the Earth's atmosphere.

Once in orbit, the shuttle uses a number of tiny gas jet engines for simple moves. It has powerful manoeuvring engines however to help it to do more difficult tasks like slowing down for re-entry, or meeting another craft which is in orbit.

The mid-section of the shuttle orbiter is a huge cargo bay, capable of carrying large satellites into orbit. Some, like the European Spacelab, are complete science stations.

Some satellites have to be placed in very distant orbits – too far for the shuttle to reach. In these cases the shuttle astronauts put the satellite in Earth orbit, and a special solid fuel rocket engine then pushes it out to its new position.

This is also how the shuttle will launch future planetary probes. The probe and its rocket engine will be carried by the shuttle to Earth orbit, and positioned. When the probe is in the correct position its rocket engine will be fired, to push the craft out from Earth and on to its new destination.

The shuttle in space

As well as putting objects into orbit, the shuttle can also collect faulty satellites and return them to Earth for repair, then replace them in orbit later.

A typical shuttle mission lasts a week or more. An immense variety of work and experiments is packed into this time. It's even possible for some schools to have experiments flown on the shuttle, in what's called a 'getaway' special. Not long ago, it would have cost tens of millions of pounds for such projects.

The beauty of the shuttle (or Space Transportation System, as NASA calls it) is that the orbiter can be used over and over again, keeping the costs low. Some day it is even possible that space tourists may do an Earth orbit in a specially converted space bus!

Once its job in orbit is done, the shuttle returns to Earth. Previous manned craft had heat shields, which burnt off slowly to carry away the fiery heat of re-entry from the crews. The shuttle orbiter is covered by a special insulation which sheds heat so rapidly that one side can be very hot indeed, and the other cool enough to touch. In this way the shuttle passes safely through the upper atmosphere, ready for landing.

Back in the dense atmosphere, the shuttle becomes a huge glider, because its engines have no fuel. By careful navigation and flight path planning, the shuttle returns to Earth on a landing strip – just like an aircraft. Then it is checked and made like new again – for its next journey into space.

The shuttle returns to Earth

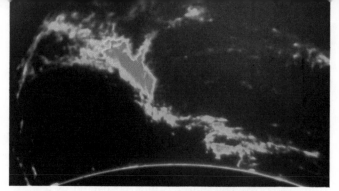

A cloud of gas shoots out from the Sun

Sun

Spacecraft have not only given us spectacular views of the planets, they have also been used to study the stars and galaxies. Our own star is the Sun and we have been able to obtain spectacular views of it both from the US manned space station Skylab, and from later unmanned craft.

The Sun may look small in our sky, but it is a really huge globe of gas 1.4 million kilometres across. Most of the Sun is hydrogen, and the temperature and pressure is so great at its centre that nuclear fusion takes place. This is what powers the Sun – a mighty nuclear core.

In the Sun, hydrogen atoms are welded together to form helium. While this is happening, a tiny amount of mass is converted to energy, which streams out, causing the Sun to shine.

Because it is gaseous, and spins once in twenty seven days, the Sun often suffers massive explosions on its surface but we are too far away to suffer serious damage from its disturbances. Spacecraft and astronauts are not so lucky. They have to take special precautions to avoid the harmful effects of solar radiation, which can destroy sensitive electronic devices and even more sensitive living tissue.

Cities in Space

In the not-too-distant future, vehicles like the space shuttle will take sections of huge space cities into orbit, and even whole colonies.

Some will take the form of giant wheels, slowly spinning to provide gravity around the rim. Here people will live and work, and may never perhaps return to planet Earth. The first steps have already been taken on a path which may some day take us to the nearer stars.

Although we can't visit the stars just yet, there is still a lot to see and explore in the sky. When there's a clear night, why not go out and try some sky-watching yourself?

One artist's idea of a space city

INDEX